At Night

Jonathan Bean

Farrar, Straus and Giroux • New York

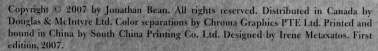

10 9 8 7 6 5 4 3 2 1

www.fsgkidsbooks.com

Library of Congress Cataloging-in-Publication Data
Bean, Jonathan, date.
    At night / Jonathan Bean.— 1st ed.
      p. cm.
    Summary: A sleepless city girl imagines what it would be like to get away from snoring
family members and curl up alone with one's thoughts in the cool night air under wide-
open skies.
    ISBN-13: 978-0-374-30446-1
    ISBN-10: 0-374-30446-7
    [1. Sleep—Fiction. 2. Night—Fiction.] I. Title.
PZ7.B3664 Asl 2007
[E]—dc22

                                                    2006048403

For my mother

At night,
after her brother
and sister went to bed,

long after her parents whispered
"Good night, happy dreams!"
and went to sleep,

she lay

in her dark room,

AWAKE.

Listening to her family sleep,
she heard her mother and father,

her sister and brother's quiet breathing.

She lay thinking alone and couldn't
close her eyes and couldn't sleep.

Then she felt a breeze

coming from the window.

Blowing over the windowsill,
it sank to the floor, drifted over her feet,
across the room,
through the door and up the stairs.
And she followed it with . . .

pillows,

a sheet,

and her blanket.

Up one stairway,
and then another,

and on to the roof, where the
small breeze joined the cool night air.

She lay in her bed
on her house in the city,

in the night, under the sky.

She thought about the wide world
all around her and smiled.

She looked up,
breathed, closed her eyes . . .

and slept.